OVERCOMING ADVERSITY: SHARING THE AMERICAN DREAM

KEVIN GARNETT

South Huntington Pub. Lib.
145 Pidgeon Hill Rd.
Huntington Sta., N.Y. 11746

MASON CREST PUBLISHERS
PHILADELPHIA

OVERCOMING ADVERSITY:
SHARING THE AMERICAN DREAM

Charles Barkley
Halle Berry
Cesar Chavez
Kenny Chesney
George Clooney
Johnny Depp
Tony Dungy
Jermaine Dupri
Jennifer Garner
Kevin Garnett
John B. Herrington
Salma Hayek
Vanessa Hudgens
Samuel L. Jackson

Norah Jones
Martin Lawrence
Bruce Lee
Eva Longoria
Malcolm X
Carlos Mencia
Chuck Norris
Barack Obama
Rosa Parks
Bill Richardson
Russell Simmons
Carrie Underwood
Modern American
  Indian Leaders

KEVIN GARNETT

JAMIE FEDORKO

MASON CREST PUBLISHERS
PHILADELPHIA

ABOUT CROSS-CURRENTS

When you see this logo, turn to the Cross-Currents section at the back of the book. The Cross-Currents features explore connections between people, places, events, and ideas.

Produced by OTTN Publishing, Stockton, New Jersey

Mason Crest Publishers
370 Reed Road
Broomall, PA 19008
www.masoncrest.com

Copyright © 2009 by Mason Crest Publishers. All rights reserved.
Printed and bound in the United States.

First printing

1 3 5 7 9 8 6 4 2

Library of Congress Cataloging-in-Publication Data

Fedorko, Jamie.
  Kevin Garnett / Jamie Fedorko.
    p. cm. — (Sharing the American dream : overcoming adversity)
  Includes bibliographical references.
  ISBN 978-1-4222-0575-4 (hardcover) — ISBN 978-1-4222-0746-8 (pbk.)
  1. Garnett, Kevin, 1976—Juvenile literature. 2. Basketball players—United States—Biography—Juvenile literature. I. Title.
  GV884.G37F43 2008
  796.323092—dc22
    [B]
                                            2008032740

TABLE OF CONTENTS

Chapter One: "Anything Is Possible"	**6**
Chapter Two: "Mr. Basketball"	**12**
Chapter Three: "Da Kid" Becomes "Da Man"	**19**
Chapter Four: All Things Must Pass	**27**
Chapter Five: "The Big Three"	**36**
Cross-Currents	**46**
Chronology	**54**
Accomplishments/Awards	**55**
Further Reading	**56**
Internet Resources	**56**
Glossary	**57**
Chapter Notes	**58**
Index	**62**

CHAPTER ONE

"ANYTHING IS POSSIBLE"

The crowd at Boston's TD Banknorth Garden grew increasingly delirious as the night of June 17, 2008, wore on. The hometown Celtics were playing the Los Angeles Lakers for the championship of the National Basketball Association (NBA). The Celtics led the best-of-seven series, three games to two, and they completely dominated Game 6. Boston took a 29-point lead into the fourth quarter and never looked back. When the horn sounded to end the game, the Celtics owned a dominating 131–92 victory—and an NBA championship. Celtics players and fans stormed onto the court to celebrate.

The Celtics were the league's most successful franchise, but it had been a long time—more than 20 years—since Boston last stood atop the NBA. The Celtics' 6'11" forward had also been waiting a long time for a championship. Kevin Garnett was in his 13th season in the NBA, though this was his first year in a Celtics uniform. As the riotous celebration unfolded on the floor of the Garden, a TV camera captured a compelling image: Kevin Garnett, covered in sweat, was on his hands and knees at center court, repeatedly kissing the Celtics' leprechaun logo.

After a few moments, Kevin rose to his feet and joined ABC's Michele Tafoya for an interview among hundreds of noisy fans.

"Anything Is Possible" 7

Kevin Garnett reacts to a basket during Game 6 of the NBA Finals, June 17, 2008. Behind Kevin's 26 points and 14 rebounds, the Boston Celtics won the game—and the championship.

His excitement erupted as he shouted, "Anything is possible! Anything is possible!"

"I Got My Own"

On the court, Kevin bumped into Celtics legend Bill Russell. "I got my own. I got my own," Kevin told the 11-time NBA champion as the two hugged. "I hope we made you proud."

"You sure did," the Hall of Famer replied.

With the NBA Finals victory over the Lakers, Kevin Garnett became part of Boston Celtics lore, joining past champions such as Bill Russell, Bob Cousy, John Havlicek, Larry Bird, and Kevin McHale. Kevin also silenced his critics. Over the years, some people had begun to view Kevin as one of the greatest NBA players never to win a championship. Some even questioned his ability to play under pressure. "Put simply, Garnett shrinks from pressure more times than he comes through," said Bill Simmons of ESPN just days before the Celtics clinched the championship.

None of that mattered now. One of Kevin's dreams had come true: he was a champion. In his televised postgame press conference, Kevin summed it up perfectly, saying, "Other than my kid being born, this has got to be the happiest day of my life."

Kevin's road to the top had been a long one, with many setbacks. After 12 seasons as a member of the Minnesota Timberwolves, he had been traded in the summer of 2007 to the Boston Celtics. He joined longtime Boston forward Paul Pierce and newly acquired guard Ray Allen in a quest to win the 17th NBA championship in the Celtics' storied history. After finishing the regular season with the NBA's best record, Boston won grueling playoff series against the Atlanta Hawks, the Cleveland Cavaliers, and the Detroit Pistons to win the Eastern Conference crown. This set up a showdown with the Los Angeles Lakers, the Western Conference champions.

The matchup was highly anticipated for several reasons. First, it featured the two NBA franchises with the most titles. Over the years, Boston had captured 16 championships; the Lakers, 14. Second, the Lakers were a young team but boasted arguably the best player in the game: Kobe Bryant, who had garnered league Most Valuable Player honors for 2008. Then there was the Celtics' incredible 2007–08 turnaround. The team had been horrendous the previous season, finishing with the second-worst record in the NBA. As Mike Kahn of FOX Sports noted on the eve of the Finals:

READ MORE
The Celtics and Lakers have met many times for the NBA championship. For details on their rivalry, turn to page 46.

> There is this amazing transformation designed by Celtics general manager Danny Ainge, altering the quicksand course of youth around All-Star Paul Pierce last summer by trading for one of the great shooters of all-time in guard Ray Allen. He followed that up with the acquisition of Kevin Garnett, one of the most complete frontcourt players to ever grace the game.

An Outstanding Series

For Kevin Garnett, being known as one of the greatest players in the game had been satisfying, but winning a championship was far more important. Throughout his career, Kevin had been known as an unselfish player who worked harder than anyone in the league on both offense and defense. Unlike the flashy Los Angeles Lakers, Kevin's Celtics had reached the Finals by focusing on

Kevin Garnett

defense and strong team play. "The defense is our backbone," Kevin noted. "When you see us beat teams and beat teams bad it's because we play defense for 48 minutes and we put our offensive game together to go with it."

Throughout the six-game series against Los Angeles, Kevin—the NBA's 2008 Defensive Player of the Year—was a force on defense. He led Boston in rebounding, averaging 13 boards per game, and he blocked a total of six shots. He also made large contributions on offense, averaging more than 18 points per game and dropping 26 in the decisive Game 6. Teammate Paul

Kevin Garnett receives a trophy as the NBA's Defensive Player of the Year, April 22, 2008.

Pierce received MVP honors for the Finals, but many would argue that Kevin Garnett's energy, hard work, and consistent play propelled his team to victory—not only in the Finals, but all season long.

Kevin Garnett had laid the foundation for his outstanding play in the Finals, and for his NBA championship, many years before. From his childhood in the quiet suburbs of Mauldin, South Carolina, to his senior year of high school in Chicago, Kevin had lived and breathed basketball.

> **READ MORE**
> Winning an NBA championship was particularly sweet for Paul Pierce, the 2008 Finals MVP. To find out why, see page 47.

CHAPTER TWO

"MR. BASKETBALL"

Kevin Maurice Garnett was born on May 19, 1976, in Greenville, South Carolina, to Shirley Garnett and O'Lewis McCullough. Kevin's parents never married, and when Shirley Garnett did marry, young Kevin and his new stepfather, Ernest Irby, didn't get along. One of the biggest causes of conflict was basketball. Ernest never supported his stepson's passion for the game, and when Kevin asked him to put up a basketball hoop, he refused.

Kevin was forced to be responsible at a young age. His family—which included an older sister, Sonya, and a younger sister, Ashley—was very poor. Kevin had to help put food on the table. While most kids were out playing with their friends, Kevin was usually working. Sometimes he bagged groceries, other times he cleaned restaurant bathrooms, as he told *HOOP* magazine:

> I've always had a job. In fairness to myself, I had no choice but to be responsible. I had to. I had to work, you know? And I've had more than some jobs in my life. More than a couple. I had no choice.

When he wasn't working, however, Kevin was focused on one thing: basketball. "All he did was talk about basketball," childhood friend Baron Franks once told reporter Ellen Tomson. "And every time you saw him, he had a ball. Sun up. Sun down. Up and down the street. All day long."

The Family Moves

When Kevin was 12 years old, his mother decided to move the family 10 miles southeast of their Greenville home, to the small city of Mauldin. Shirley Garnett wanted her children to live in a safe place and attend good schools. "I'm an advocate of education," she revealed in a 2008 book. "Always saved for my children's college educations. My plans were for [Kevin] to go to school."

Kevin himself remained focused on basketball, however. As he recalled in 2006, "When I didn't have a friend, when I was lonely, I always knew I could grab that orange pill and go hoop. If things weren't going right, I could make a basket and feel better."

When he arrived in Mauldin, Kevin found a few close friends, like Jamie "Bug" Peters, still his best friend today. He also found a community that loved basketball as much as he did. As soon as Kevin took up organized basketball, it became clear that he had a true talent.

When he was growing up, Kevin Garnett worked obsessively on his basketball skills.

From the Streets to the Gym: A Star Is Born

For years, Kevin had been working hard on local playgrounds to improve his game. But it wasn't until his freshman year at Mauldin High School that he first started playing organized basketball. His coach, James Fisher, was impressed from the day they met. "I knew he was gifted the first time I saw him on the court," Fisher told the online magazine *Salon* in 2000. "I'd bust him at basketball practice, I mean really bust him, and then he'd go to the park and play basketball there. He'd leave one practice and go practice again. I never saw someone so obsessed."

As a high school freshman, Kevin stood 6'6" tall, and he was clearly a talented athlete. Still, there were holes in his game because he had never gotten good coaching. In his first year at Mauldin High, Kevin concentrated on rebounding, blocking shots, and playing defense, and he quickly became a defensive force. In the summer before his sophomore year, Kevin decided it was time to improve his offensive game. He played Amateur Athletic Union (AAU) basketball and worked harder than ever. Recalled Stan Hopkins, his school's athletic director, "I don't think I ever saw a kid enjoy playing that much. When you have that kind of talent and work ethic, it turns you into a super player."

Prom night: High school senior Kevin Garnett and his date, June 1995.

Kevin wasn't interested in being an individual star, however. Basketball is a team game, and he always played to help his team win. He passed the ball just as much as he shot it, and he played defense as hard as he played offense. "Kevin could have averaged 30 points a game—easy, " recalled his AAU coach, Darren "Bull" Gazaway. "But he didn't. He probably averaged about 18 points. He would pass, set up other players. Just loved to play the game."

And crowds loved to watch Kevin play. He was tall, fast, skilled, and passionate. Eventually scouts from colleges all over the country began to notice. In his junior year at Mauldin, Kevin averaged 27 points, 17 rebounds, and 7 blocked shots per game. He led his team to the title game of the state basketball championships. And he was named South Carolina's "Mr. Basketball," the award given to the most outstanding high school player in the state.

After his outstanding junior season, Kevin looked forward to an even more dominant senior year. But an ugly incident would prevent him from playing any more basketball at Mauldin.

Chicago-Bound

One day in May 1994, a white student at Mauldin was badly beaten. There are numerous versions of what happened. In the end, however, Kevin Garnett and four others were blamed for the incident. Kevin was arrested and charged with second-degree lynching. In general usage the term *lynching* calls to mind America's racially troubled past, when mobs of whites (especially in the South) sometimes seized and murdered African Americans as a means of racial intimidation. Under South Carolina law, however, second-degree lynching is a common charge. It is brought when two or more people inflict bodily harm on another person that does not result in death.

Kevin Garnett

The news spread like wildfire. Every newspaper and TV station told the story of the star basketball player who'd been arrested. But no matter what the reports said, Kevin insisted he was merely an innocent bystander. In the end, all the charges against Kevin were dropped as he qualified for a pretrial intervention program for first-time offenders.

During this difficult period in his life, Kevin learned important lessons about overcoming adversity, and he found out who his real friends were. As he told writer Frank Clancy:

> At the time I thought I had amps of friends. I thought everybody was my boy. When you get in trouble, or you go broke, that's when you find out who your boys are. You've got something like basketball or a nice job, people always want to be around you. Once you mess up? They're gone. That's what I learned.

In the aftermath of her son's legal troubles, Shirley Garnett decided that it would be best if Kevin got a fresh start. She moved Kevin and his sister Ashley to Chicago. There her son could have a chance to play at the famed Farragut Academy under Coach William "Wolf"

Farragut Academy's Kevin Garnett goes up for a layup, 1995. Kevin starred for the Chicago basketball powerhouse in his senior year of high school.

Nelson. Nelson had coached Kevin a year earlier, during a Nike summer league.

Nelson drilled his players relentlessly in the fundamentals of basketball. But, recognizing Kevin Garnett's unique talents, he also unleashed the 6'10" senior. Nelson made it clear to Kevin that there was nothing wrong with putting up big numbers. And Kevin did just that, averaging 25.2 points, 17.9 rebounds, 6.7 assists, and 6.5 blocked shots per game in his season with Farragut. In the process, he led the team to a 28–2 record and a trip to the Class AA state quarterfinals. Kevin was again named "Mr. Basketball," this time for the state of Illinois.

> **READ MORE**
>
> Kevin Garnett is among a handful of players who have gone on to NBA stardom after being drafted right out of high school. To find out about some of the others, see page 48.

NBA: Here I Come

During his year at Farragut, Kevin realized that his grades were a problem. He twice took the standardized academic tests given to students who plan to attend college. But both times, he failed to get a score that was high enough for a major college to be permitted to offer him a

Kevin hugs his mother, Shirley, after learning that he has been selected in the first round of the 1995 NBA draft by the Minnesota Timberwolves.

basketball scholarship. So Kevin did something no other player had done in 20 years: he entered the NBA draft straight from high school.

Many people doubted that Kevin would be able to handle the jump to the NBA. Former Boston Celtics legend and Minnesota Timberwolves executive Kevin McHale was not one of them. With the fifth pick in the 1995 NBA draft, McHale selected the high school senior, who now stood 6'11" and weighed 217 pounds.

CHAPTER THREE

"DA KID" BECOMES "DA MAN"

When Kevin Garnett announced that he wanted to go straight from high school to the NBA, there were many people who thought he simply was not ready. "First of all, Kevin Garnett is not ready to play in the NBA. He just isn't close," wrote Michael Wilbon in the *Washington Post*. "His skill level isn't high enough; he isn't savvy enough." Jay Mariotti of the *Chicago Sun-Times* couldn't have agreed more, saying, "Is Kevin Garnett ready for it all? Obviously, hell, no. It is such a fragile proposition—the thought someone could enter the NBA so young, no matter how gifted and tall and extraordinarily athletic, and be better off in the long term."

The debate about whether or not Kevin was ready for the NBA was more about whether any teenager—not just Kevin Garnett—was physically, mentally, and emotionally capable of playing in a league of grown men. Furthermore, many people were upset that Kevin was choosing to forgo the chance to attend college. But Kevin felt that he needed to help his mother and sisters become more financially secure.

Sports Illustrated highlighted the debate by placing Kevin Garnett on the cover of its June 26, 1995, issue. The headline read "Ready or Not . . ."

To make sure he would be ready, Kevin worked extremely hard over the summer months. He had something to prove to sportswriters and fellow NBA players who had begun referring to him as "Da Kid" because of his youth and inexperience.

Growing Pains

Kevin began his rookie season of 1995–96 as a bench player for the Timberwolves. He usually came into games to give forwards Christian Laettner and Tom Gugliotta a rest. Coach Bill Blair and general manager Kevin McHale, believing that Kevin needed time to adjust to the NBA game, were determined not to ask too much of him too soon. Also, at less than 220 pounds, Kevin was skinny by the standards of NBA big men. Blair and McHale didn't want him to be pushed around.

During the first half of the season, Kevin averaged only about six points and four rebounds per game. Still, fans began noticing his potential as he wowed crowds with soaring dunks and blocked shots.

Midway through the season and with the Timberwolves strug-

Nineteen-year-old rookie Kevin Garnett dunks over Chris Childs of the New York Nets, December 6, 1995. Kevin displayed flashes of brilliance during his first season with the Minnesota Timberwolves.

gling, McHale fired Coach Blair and replaced him with Phil "Flip" Saunders. Soon, Kevin Garnett was starting—and making an impact. By the end of the season he had raised his averages to 10.4 points, 6.3 rebounds, and 1.6 blocked shots per game—earning a spot on the All-Rookie Second Team. Even though he had improved over the course of the year, Kevin confessed that his rookie season had been extremely tough.

The $126-Million Man

Kevin began coming into his own in his second NBA season, 1996–97. He averaged 17 points, 8 rebounds, and 2.1 blocked shots per game. "Da Kid" also became the youngest player to be voted an NBA All-Star since Magic Johnson in 1980. More important, the Timberwolves reached the playoffs for the first time in franchise history, although they lost to the Houston Rockets in the first round. To top off his success, Kevin was named to *Newsweek*'s list of the "100 Most Influential People of the Next Decade," in the magazine's April 27, 1997, issue. The Timberwolves knew they had a budding superstar in Kevin Garnett, but there was one problem: They had to make sure the 21-year-old remained a member of the team for the long haul.

The team had a good nucleus consisting of rookie guard Stephon Marbury, star forward Tom Gugliotta, and Kevin Garnett. But general manager Kevin McHale saw Kevin Garnett as the future of the franchise. With that in mind, he offered Kevin a contract worth $102 million over five years. Kevin's agent, Eric Fleisher, instructed his client to turn down the offer. Fleisher assured Kevin that he would be able to get even more money when he became a free agent after the following season.

Timberwolves owner Glen Taylor didn't want to risk losing Kevin Garnett. Just a month before the start of the 1997–98 season, Taylor offered Kevin a six-year, $126 million contract. Kevin accepted the deal, which at the time was the biggest contract in the history of any sport.

Garnett Makes the T-Wolves a Threat

As the 1997–98 season got under way, expectations were high among fans of the Minnesota Timberwolves. The T-Wolves did not disappoint. Minnesota compiled a record of 45–37, the first winning season in franchise history.

Kevin Garnett shone. The season had started with his critics—mostly NBA owners—calling him greedy, selfish, and immature because of his contract dispute. But, under intense pressure to prove he was worth $126 million, Kevin delivered. He averaged 18.5 points, 9.6 rebounds, and 4.2 assists per game, all career highs. Kevin earned a starting position on the Western Conference All-Star team.

After the regular season came to a close, the T-Wolves geared up for their first-round playoff matchup against the Seattle Supersonics. Seattle had finished the season tied for the second best record in the Western Conference. After losing badly in Game 1, the Timberwolves came back, taking the second and third games behind the solid play of Kevin Garnett. Facing elimination in the best-of-five series, the veteran Sonics responded, winning Game 4 and Game 5 to advance. The Timberwolves had turned in a credible season, making the playoffs for the second consecutive year. Still, Kevin, the team, and their fans expected more.

A True Superstar

Everyone would have to wait a long time to see whether Minnesota could reach the next level. NBA owners were concerned that player salaries were becoming too high—and Kevin Garnett's $126 million deal was often cited as evidence of this.

Western Conference All-Star Kevin Garnett grabs a rebound as the Eastern Conference's Chris Webber looks on, February 7, 1997. The East won the game, 132–120.

The owners demanded that the players accept a limit on the size of each team's payroll. When the players union refused, the owners decided to lock the players out. No games would be played, and no practices held, until an agreement was signed.

It wasn't until January 1999 that the two sides reached a compromise and NBA games resumed. The lockout-shortened regular season would include only 50 games rather than the usual 82.

Blocking out the criticism that had been leveled at him because of his huge contract, Kevin Garnett turned in another excellent season. He averaged more than 20 points and 10 rebounds per game.

The Timberwolves finished with a record of 25–25 and once again made the playoffs. However, without point guard Stephon Marbury—who had been traded away 18 games into the season—the T-Wolves experienced more postseason frustrations. Minnesota suffered its third consecutive first-round playoff defeat, this time to the eventual NBA champion San Antonio Spurs.

Even though his team was spinning its wheels, Kevin was now a true superstar. "Who would have ever thought that a high school player would come in and change everything?" NBA legend and analyst Bill Walton asked. "But here was Kevin Garnett, who came from nothing and all of a sudden has become as great a player as there is." Kevin couldn't help noticing this kind of praise. But he was more concerned with winning. "Da Kid" had become "Da Man," and he was respected across the league.

More Playoff Problems

Kevin Garnett and the Minnesota Timberwolves began the 1999–2000 season expecting the best. The team had acquired point guard Terrell Brandon in the Marbury trade the season before, and Brandon now appeared to be comfortable playing with Kevin Garnett. The team also drafted Wally Szczerbiak, a star forward in college and a proven scorer. As the season progressed, so did the team. Minnesota finished the regular season with a record of 50–32. It was the first 50-win season in franchise history.

Despite their excellent regular-season showing, the T-Wolves again lost in the first round of the playoffs, this time to the Portland Trail Blazers. Kevin had done his best to help his team advance, averaging 18.8 points, 10.8 rebounds, and 8.8 assists

"Da Kid" Becomes "Da Man"

in the series. But Kevin's disappointment at another early exit from the postseason would soon pale in the face of a terrible tragedy.

The Death of Malik Sealy

Growing up, Kevin Garnett had idolized NBA player Malik Sealy. Years later, the two became teammates in Minnesota and formed a very close friendship. On May 20, 2000, Sealy helped celebrate Kevin's 24th birthday

> **READ MORE**
> Dying in the prime of life isn't something that people expect to happen to great athletes. But Malik Sealy was just one of three active NBA players who died between 1993 and 2000. For details, see page 49.

(Above) Malik Sealy in action for the Minnesota Timberwolves, April 2000. (Right) Pallbearers carry Sealy's casket, May 26, 2000. Kevin Garnett is at top left, wearing sunglasses.

with him. On his way home that night, Sealy was killed when his car was hit head-on by a drunk driver driving on the wrong side of the road. He was only 30 years old.

Kevin Garnett was devastated by the loss of his good friend. But Kevin had responsibilities to keep—including his commitment to play for Team USA at the 2000 Summer Olympics in Sydney, Australia. Kevin couldn't afford to become paralyzed by his grief. "I know [Malik's] gone to a better place and that's what's keeping me so strong," Kevin revealed.

> **READ MORE**
>
> For information about how the U.S. men's basketball team fared at the 2000 Summer Olympics, turn to page 50.

CHAPTER FOUR

ALL THINGS MUST PASS

In each of his first five seasons in Minnesota, Kevin Garnett had improved his scoring and rebounding averages. Along the way, he had developed into one of the NBA's top players. With the exception of his rookie season, Kevin had been selected to the All-Star team every year.

The Timberwolves, too, had shown steady improvement during the regular season. But the playoffs were a different story. The T-Wolves had yet to advance past the first round of the playoffs.

In 2000–2001, Kevin Garnett turned in another outstanding season. He averaged 22 points, 11.4 rebounds, 5 assists, and 1.8 blocked shots per game. He again made the All-Star and NBA All-Defensive teams. He again took his team to the playoffs. The result, unfortunately, was the same: a first-round playoff defeat to the San Antonio Spurs.

An All-Star Off the Court

While many people admired Kevin's abilities on the court, they were unaware of how involved he was in charitable activities off the court. Kevin visited sick kids in hospitals on a regular basis. He gave large sums of money to charities such as the Boys and Girls Clubs of America. And during the 2001–02 season, he

Kevin Garnett mingles with students in the tech center at Patrick Henry High School in Minneapolis, Minnesota, March 20, 2006. Kevin had bought all the computers through his 4XL charitable foundation.

launched 4XL—For Excellence and Leadership—which took his off-court work to new heights.

During the 2002 NBA All-Star weekend, Kevin announced the new foundation. He described it as a program to help minority high school and college students prepare for careers in business. The program has three parts: guidance in business, leadership, and technology. On his personal Web site, Kevin admitted that he too could use some help in these areas:

READ MORE

Kevin Garnett has been extremely generous in supporting charitable causes. One example: his $1.2 million donation to help the victims of Hurricane Katrina. For details, see page 51.

> So many young people hope for a bright future but need the roadmap to help them pursue their

passions and realize their dreams. One of my passions is apparel, and I am learning how to be a successful entrepreneur. 4XL provides opportunities for young people to gain exposure, guidance, and access to the business world, and I am excited to learn along with them.

At 25 years old, Kevin Garnett had already made a big mark both on and off the court. Kevin was, as writer Scoop Jackson noted several years later, a "man who had multimillions of reasons to disassociate himself from his community and the hands and prying eyes of the general public, but hasn't. Who in a '97 *Newsweek* article reluctantly admitted that he was going to be one of the 100 most influential people (not athletes) in the world by the year 2010."

Different Season, Same Ending

Kevin finished the 2001–02 season with outstanding stats. He averaged more than 21 points, 12 rebounds, and 5 assists per game. Kevin made the NBA All-Star team and All-Defensive team once again. And once again, the Timberwolves enjoyed a successful regular season, finishing with a record of 50–32. But the team continued to come up small in the postseason. In 2002 they were dispatched in the first round of the playoffs by the Dallas Mavericks.

Kevin's 2002–03 season was his best yet. He averaged a career-high 23 points, 13.4 rebounds, and 6 assists per game. Kevin finished second to San Antonio Spurs big man Tim Duncan in voting for NBA Most Valuable Player honors.

Behind Kevin's dominant play, the Timberwolves finished the regular season with a franchise-record 51 wins. They faced the Los Angeles Lakers in the first round of the playoffs. Incredibly,

Kevin Garnett slams the ball home in a December 2002 game against the Chicago Bulls. The 2002–03 season would turn out to be Kevin's finest to date. But his Timberwolves were bounced in the first round of the playoffs for the seventh consecutive time.

the T-Wolves again suffered a first-round defeat, just as they had in the previous six years.

Not surprisingly, some sportswriters and fans blamed Minnesota's best player, Kevin Garnett, for the team's postseason futility. Some critics began to question his ability to come through in the clutch. Timberwolves officials, however, wanted to make sure Kevin stayed in Minnesota.

Another $100 Million, Another Supporting Cast

Fresh off their seventh consecutive first-round playoff loss, the Timberwolves were still hopeful. Instead of rebuilding the franchise with young players, they gave their star, Kevin Garnett, a new five-year contract extension—worth $100 million—and brought in veteran guards Sam Cassell and Latrell Sprewell to play alongside him. Kevin knew that the 2003–04 season would be his best chance yet at winning a championship. He told the Web site InsideHoops, "Anybody mess this up, it's going to be us. We're excited."

On a preseason conference call with members of the media, coach Flip Saunders noted that, with the addition of established stars like Cassell and Sprewell, the Timberwolves wouldn't always have to rely on Kevin Garnett to carry them:

> Kevin McHale and myself sat down along with our owner and said now it's time to bring in people that can make K.G. better, to take pressure off of him. So, when you look at that, you look at people that know how to win, that know how to play in situations and can take pressure off and have the ability to make big shots down the stretch.

For his part, Cassell could not have been more impressed with "the Big Ticket," as Kevin Garnett was now known. "I've never met

Sam Cassell (right) celebrates a playoff victory over the Denver Nuggets with Timberwolves teammate Kevin Garnett, April 30, 2004. During the 2003–04 season, the T-Wolves finally advanced past the first round of the playoffs.

anyone like him. . . . Ticket, hell, Ticket got me coming—and wanting to come—to practice," Cassell said. "I've never liked practice. But since I've been [in Minnesota], seeing what he does everyday, how hard he works everyday, man, psssh . . . and I'm supposed to be the veteran with two [championship] rings, right?"

An MVP and a Title Run

All the excitement was fine, but winning was better. And win the Timberwolves did. They finished the 2003–04 regular season with a record of 58–24, second best in the NBA. After posting career highs of 24.2 points, 13.9 rebounds, and 2.2 blocks per game, Kevin Garnett was voted the NBA's Most Valuable Player for the season. He was also a unanimous selection to the NBA All-Defensive team, the fifth year he was voted to the squad.

Kevin appreciated the recognition as league MVP, but as usual he was focused only on helping the T-Wolves win a championship. As he said on Minnesota Public Radio, "My goals are a lot bigger than just an individual award, but if I get—when I get—that big gold [championship] trophy, that's really going to solidify my journey."

And he was getting closer. In round one of the 2004 NBA playoffs, Kevin's Timberwolves faced the Denver Nuggets, and they finally won a postseason series. Kevin averaged 25.8 points, 14.8 rebounds, 7 assists, and 2 blocked shots per game for the series. Afterward, Kevin couldn't hide his happiness. "I am very excited," he said. "I am not going to downplay it. I am eager to see what is on the other side."

On the other side stood Chris Webber and the Sacramento Kings. The two teams played a grueling seven-game series, but in the end Kevin's T-Wolves emerged victorious. They had earned a trip to the Western Conference Finals.

All Things Must Pass

Minnesota faced off against the Los Angeles Lakers. The NBA's defending champions, the Lakers featured a star-studded lineup that included Shaquille O'Neal and Kobe Bryant. Los Angeles took Game 1, which was played in Minnesota, by a score of 97–88. Although the T-Wolves roared back with an 89–71 Game 2 victory, the Lakers won the next two games to push Minnesota to the brink of elimination in the best-of-seven series. Behind a monster performance by Kevin Garnett—he scored 30 points and grabbed 19 rebounds—the T-Wolves won a 98–96 nail-biter in Game 5. But Minnesota's playoff run came to

> **READ MORE**
>
> In sports, it is often said, winning solves everything, including conflicts between teammates. This wasn't true with Los Angeles Lakers superstars Shaquille O'Neal and Kobe Bryant. The two feuded even as their team won NBA titles. See page 52 for details.

Los Angeles Lakers center Shaquille O'Neal defends Kevin Garnett during action from the NBA Western Conference Finals, May 31, 2004. Shaq and his teammates prevailed in the series, four games to two.

an end in the next game in Los Angeles, where the Lakers banged out a 96–90 victory to win the series, four games to two.

Kevin had an excellent postseason, averaging 24.3 points and 14.6 rebounds per game throughout the playoffs. "I got a taste of the Western Conference Finals," he told reporters after the T-Wolves had been eliminated by Los Angeles, "but it's like [Latrell Sprewell] said in the locker room. It doesn't mean anything if you don't win it all. . . . We've just got to use this as experience and add a couple of pieces and go from there."

Next Stop: Boston

Kevin's assessment that his team just needed a couple more pieces proved overly optimistic. After reaching the Western Conference Finals in 2004, Minnesota missed the playoffs entirely for the next three seasons.

Veteran Boston Celtics star Paul Pierce (left) poses with new teammates Kevin Garnett and Ray Allen, July 2007.

T-Wolves owner Glen Taylor decided that his team needed to rebuild. In a blockbuster trade that brought up-and-coming star Al Jefferson and several other players to the Timberwolves, Kevin Garnett was dealt to the Boston Celtics in the summer of 2007. Boston also traded for star guard Ray Allen that summer. The two newcomers joined a team that already included high-scoring forward Paul Pierce, making Boston a preseason favorite to contend for an NBA championship.

CHAPTER FIVE

"THE BIG THREE"

The off-season moves made by the Boston Celtics in the summer of 2007 were greeted with immediate approval by Celts fans and players. With All-Stars Kevin Garnett and Ray Allen added to Boston's lineup, high-scoring forward Paul Pierce—himself an All-Star—would have a lot more support on the floor. "This is a tremendous day," the 30-year-old Pierce told the media after the Garnett trade. "I feel like a rookie again."

For his part, Kevin Garnett was ecstatic about playing in Boston. "This is probably my best opportunity at winning a ring," Kevin told reporters. "It was a no-brainer."

Boston sportswriters and fans began referring to the combination of Pierce, Allen, and Garnett as "the Big Three." The nickname recalled a glorious era in Celtics history—the 1980s, when the team won three NBA titles in six years. Those championship clubs had been led by another trio dubbed "the Big Three": Larry Bird, Kevin McHale, and Robert Parish.

Boston Celtics general manager Danny Ainge thought the comparison between Pierce, Allen, and Garnett and the original Big Three was a bit premature. "These guys will never be the Big Three," Ainge told ESPN, "until they win."

"The Big Three" 37

Great expectations: On the eve of the 2007–08 NBA season, Boston's new "Big Three"—Paul Pierce, Kevin Garnett, and Ray Allen—reminded some longtime Celtics fans of the legendary trio of Larry Bird, Kevin McHale, and Robert Parish.

Starting Strong

On November 2, 2007, the Boston Celtics took the court for the first regular-season game with Kevin Garnett on the club. Boston's new superstar did not disappoint. Facing the Washington Wizards, Kevin scored 22 points, grabbed 20 rebounds, and handed out 5 assists as the Celtics won the game, 103–83. Coach Doc Rivers told reporters in a press conference after the game that Kevin "was so hyped up tonight, his first shot almost broke the backboard. He was terrific."

Paced by the Big Three, the Boston Celtics were an unstoppable force during the 2007–08 regular season.

Kevin, however, wasn't satisfied with the 20-point win. "We didn't execute like we know we can," he said, "so we still have some work to do."

Boston reeled off seven more wins before losing its first game of the season. And the victories kept coming. When the Celtics beat the Los Angeles Lakers on December 30, Boston's record stood at 26–3.

Kevin Garnett's offensive stats weren't as high as in previous years—he would finish the season averaging less than 20 points per game for the first time in 10 seasons—but throughout the 2007–08 campaign, he helped the Celtics win. Basketball fans and sportswriters marveled at the way Kevin and the other members of the Big Three played so unselfishly together. For Kevin, the explanation was obvious: the only thing the players cared about was winning one game at a time—no matter who was the star on a given night. As he told the *Boston Herald*:

> It's about what you're able to sacrifice. I think the reason the three of us work is because we don't just talk about sacrifice, but it's something we actually exercise. It's our way of life. We put the team above everything and the wins above everything, and at the end of the day, that's all that matters.

The Importance of Defense

Over the years, NBA coaches and players have used the phrase "defense wins championships" to emphasize how important that aspect of the game is, especially since most people tend to pay more attention to offense. Kevin Garnett is known to be an exceptional defender. He is also known for his intensity and strong work ethic.

The Celtics, on the other hand, were coming off several very poor seasons and were known as a bad defensive team. Kevin helped Boston overcome this handicap. "Garnett completely altered the culture of the [Celtics]," the *Boston Herald* noted, "transforming them into one of the league's most focused teams, particularly on defense."

By January 25, 2008—going into a game with Kevin's old team, the Timberwolves—the Celtics had compiled an astounding record of 34–7. In the fourth quarter of that game, Kevin injured a muscle in his thigh, the quadriceps. He left the game but managed to return in time to make a big steal that secured another Celtics victory. But the injury kept him from playing again until February 19.

Nevertheless, the Celtics barely missed a beat. Their record stood at 41–10 after Kevin's first game back, a win over the Denver Nuggets. On March 5, with a 90–78 drubbing of the Detroit Pistons, Boston clinched a playoff spot—and there were

Kevin Garnett celebrates the Celtics' victory over his former team, the Minnesota Timberwolves, on January 25, 2008. A quadriceps injury Kevin sustained in the game would sideline him for three weeks, but Boston continued to win in his absence.

still almost six weeks left in the season. By March 14, the Celtics had clinched the Atlantic Division crown.

Boston finished the regular season at 66–16. That was the best record in the NBA for 2007–08. But, equally impressive, it represented the biggest single-season turnaround in league history: the Celtics had won only 24 games in 2006–07.

Kevin Garnett had played a key role in the Celtics' success, and his contributions didn't go unrecognized. He was named the NBA's Defensive Player of the Year. Yet all he cared about was winning the title. "Any award you're able to acquire in this league is a big deal," Kevin told reporters. "At the end of the day, it's about winning."

His teammates and coaches still made sure Kevin got the credit he deserved. "He's changed our culture defensively," head coach Doc Rivers said. "That's the most important thing, just the team part of it. Individually, he's been fantastic, but I think his presence for the team is what stood out." Thanks to Kevin Garnett, the Celtics were the best defensive team in the league during the season, and they were about to work even harder in their first playoff series against the Atlanta Hawks.

Close Calls

Very few people gave the Atlanta Hawks a chance going into their first-round series against the Celtics. Most people thought the Hawks wouldn't win a single game. Early in the series, there seemed little reason to doubt that assessment. Playing on their home court of TD Banknorth Garden, the Celtics administered two severe beatings to the Hawks, winning Game 1 by 23 points and Game 2 by 19 points.

When the series resumed in Atlanta, however, the scrappy Hawks fought back. They took Game 3 by a score of 102–93, then gritted out a 97–92 Game 4 victory to even the series.

Back in Boston, the Celtics took Game 5 by a 25-point margin. But any thought that the Hawks would now roll over was dispelled in Game 6, when Atlanta stunned the visiting Celtics, 103–100.

Boston now faced elimination in what would surely go down as one of the biggest upsets of recent years. Kevin and his teammates were determined not to let that happen. On May 4, 2008, the Celtics suffocated the Hawks at the Garden. Kevin contributed 18 points and 11 rebounds in the 99–65 blowout.

The Celtics moved into the Eastern Conference Semifinals, against the Cleveland Cavaliers and LeBron James. Again, the going was tough. Boston won all the games at the Garden but could not get a win in Cleveland. Fortunately for the Celtics, their league-best record in the regular season gave them home-court advantage throughout the playoffs. In the decisive Game 7 against the Cavaliers, Kevin scored just 13 points, but he grabbed 13 rebounds and played outstanding defense to help seal a thrilling 97–92 victory for his team.

Kevin Garnett: NBA Champion

The Celtics had an easier time in the Eastern Conference Finals than in the previous two series. They eliminated the Detroit Pistons, four games to two. In the decisive Game 6, played on Detroit's home court, Boston overcame a 10-point deficit by outscoring the Pistons 29–13 in the fourth quarter.

Now all that stood between Boston and an NBA title was the Western Conference champion Los Angeles Lakers. Many basketball observers believed that the Lakers, paced by league MVP Kobe Bryant, would prevail. In fact, before the series began, nine ESPN analysts picked the Lakers to win the series, while only one chose the Celtics.

"The Big Three"

The experts were wrong. Boston won the series, four games to two. And they put an exclamation point on the championship by defeating L.A. in Game 6 by a staggering 39 points, the largest margin of victory in NBA Finals history.

During the Celtics' championship run, Kevin Garnett put to rest any criticism that he wilted under the pressure of postseason play. He averaged 20.4 points and 10.5 rebounds for the entire 2007–08 postseason. And in the championship-clinching game against Los Angeles, he was spectacular. Writer Bill Simmons, who had

> **READ MORE**
>
> The Celtics' 2008 NBA title may have been a long time coming, but since 2001, Boston sports fans have enjoyed a bounty of championships. For details, see page 53.

Celtic celebration: Kevin Garnett, Ray Allen, and Paul Pierce with the Larry O'Brien NBA Championship Trophy, June 17, 2008.

recently criticized Kevin's ability to come through in the clutch, gushed:

> Garnett finished with 26 points and 14 rebounds and played his usual terrific defense, but, more importantly, he found his swagger again, a level of passion and intensity that's unique to him and only him. . . . Let the record show Garnett played one of his greatest games to help clinch a championship.

The Legacy

Kevin Garnett developed a passion for basketball while growing up in Mauldin, South Carolina. The skinny youngster improved

Kevin Garnett, a champion at last, enjoys the moment.

his game in Chicago during his senior year of high school and developed a reputation for being selfless and intense. His hard work enabled him to make history over and over again. He was the first person in 20 years to successfully jump to the NBA straight from high school. Then he was the highest-paid athlete in American history. Then he was an MVP. After that, he helped bring about the biggest single-season turnaround in league history en route to realizing his lifelong dream of winning an NBA championship.

Retirement from basketball may well be years away, but Kevin Garnett has already secured an impressive legacy. He is a tireless worker who drives himself to be the best, yet always remembers that basketball is a team sport, and success is measured not by individual statistics but by team championships. He is also a man who gives generously to help less fortunate members of the community. On and off the court, Kevin Garnett is a true champion.

CROSS-CURRENTS

The Lakers-Celtics Rivalry

The Los Angeles Lakers and the Boston Celtics are widely considered to be the two strongest franchises in NBA history. As of 2008, Boston had won a league-best 17 championships, and the Lakers had captured 14 titles. No other team had won even half as many.

Over the years, the Lakers and Celtics have had some epic championship battles against each other. Between 1959 and 1970, the two teams met in the NBA Finals seven times. During that era, Elgin Baylor, Jerry West, and Wilt Chamberlain were key players for the Lakers, while Bill Russell, Bob Cousy, and John Havlicek paced the Celtics. The Celtics won all seven matchups with the Lakers and dominated the NBA for the entire decade.

Los Angeles and Boston didn't meet in the Finals again until 1984, when Larry Bird led the Celtics and Magic Johnson led the Lakers. The Lakers once again lost to the Celtics. However, the Lakers won when the two teams faced each other in 1985 and 1987. Other key players in the series included James Worthy and Kareem Abdul-Jabbar for the Lakers, and Kevin McHale and Robert Parish for the Celtics.

When the Lakers and Celtics both reached the Finals in 2008, it was the 11th time the two teams had played for the NBA championship. With the Celtics' victory, they led the series nine to two.

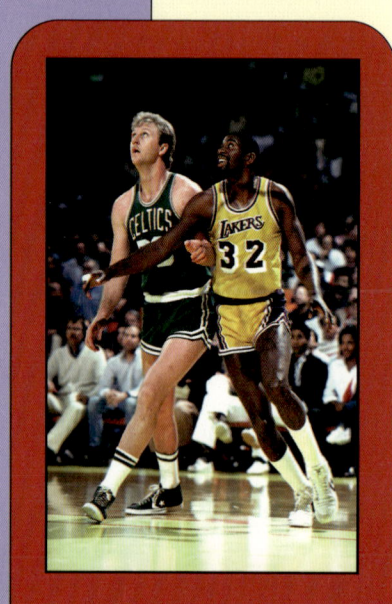

Two of basketball's all-time greats, Larry Bird of the Boston Celtics and Magic Johnson of the Los Angeles Lakers, in action from 1986.

CROSS-CURRENTS

2008 NBA Finals MVP

Paul Pierce of the Boston Celtics was named the NBA Finals MVP against the Lakers after averaging 21.8 points, 6.3 assists, and 4.5 rebounds per game during the six-game series. Pierce was in his 10th season with the Celtics, and before 2008 he had never seen his team advance past the Eastern Conference Finals. But it was the Celtics' amazing turnaround after their horrible 2006–07 season that made the 2008 championship especially sweet for Pierce. "This is unreal just [because of] where we came from a year ago, where I was at, to be here today celebrating with my teammates, putting a stamp on what a great year it was," Pierce said following the Game 6 victory.

Still, Paul Pierce has overcome greater difficulties off the basketball court. On September 25, 2000, after getting into a fight at a nightclub in Boston, Pierce was stabbed multiple times in the back, neck, and chest. Amazingly, he played every game of the 2000–01 season. And, as he told ESPN, the incident helped him put his life into perspective. "It was a shock," Pierce said. "I didn't realize how badly hurt I was until after the incident. . . . I didn't realize how much my life was in danger until after it was all over."

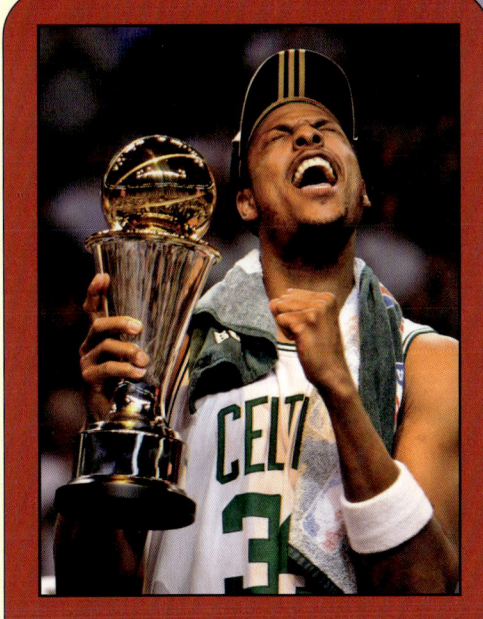

Paul Pierce rejoices as he wins the NBA Finals MVP award for 2008.

CROSS-CURRENTS

From High School to the NBA

For most NBA players, the typical route is from high school to college to the pros. College offers players the chance not only to get a degree, but also to gain valuable court experience and to develop physically. Many 18- or 19-year-olds are simply not strong enough to compete with NBA players.

Still, a few players have successfully made the jump straight from high school to the pros. In 1974, the Utah Stars of the ABA—a pro league that later merged with the NBA—drafted 6'10" center Moses Malone. Malone went on to win NBA MVP honors three times. In 1996, during the 50th anniversary of the NBA, he was named one of the league's 50 greatest players of all time.

In the 1975 NBA draft, two other high school players—Darryl Dawkins and Bill Willoughby—were picked. Neither found the success that Moses Malone enjoyed. The next high school player to be drafted was Kevin Garnett, in 1995. He was followed by Kobe Bryant and Jermaine O'Neal (both drafted in 1996); Tracy McGrady (1997); and Amare Stoudemire and LeBron James (2003). All have become NBA stars.

In the summer of 2005, however, the NBA set up an age requirement. Now teams cannot draft players right from high school.

Moses Malone, photographed after being drafted directly out of high school by the ABA's Utah Stars, August 1974.

CROSS-CURRENTS

Gone Before Their Time

Between 1993 and 2000, the NBA saw three of its bright young players die. The first was New Jersey Nets star guard Drazen Petrovic. Born in Croatia, Petrovic was one of several players who came to the NBA from Europe during the 1980s and 1990s as the league attempted to make basketball a more global game. Many of these players failed to catch on in the NBA, but Petrovic succeeded. He averaged better than 15 points per game for his career, including 22.3 points per game in his final season, 1992–93. Petrovic died on June 7, 1993, in a car accident in Germany. He was 28 years old.

A little more than a month later, on July 27, 1993, Boston Celtics captain and budding young star Reggie Lewis collapsed and died during a workout at Brandeis University. Lewis had collapsed earlier that year, during a playoff game against the Charlotte Hornets. That incident had revealed a heart condition, and Lewis was deciding whether or not to return to basketball at the time of his fatal workout. He was 27 years old when he died.

Seven years later, on May 20, 2000, Malik Sealy of the Timberwolves died in a car accident. Sealy was 30.

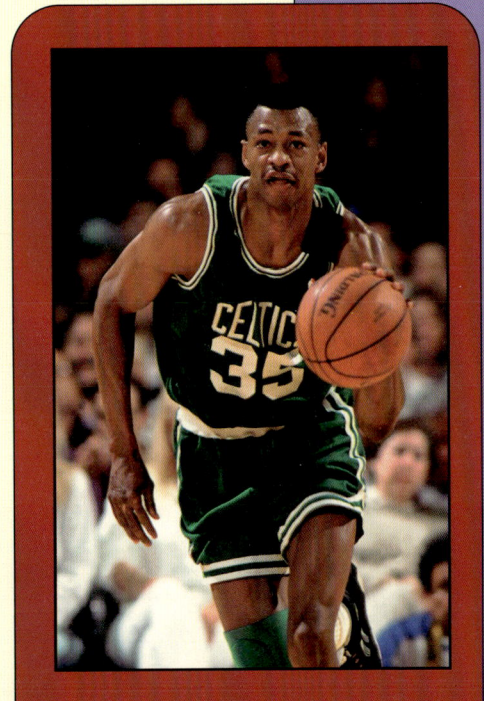

Reggie Lewis in action in January 1993, only months before his death.

CROSS-CURRENTS

Team USA at the 2000 Summer Olympics

The 2000 Summer Olympics were held in Sydney, Australia. The U.S. men's basketball team consisted of Kevin Garnett, Allan Houston, Alonzo Mourning, Antonio McDyess, Gary Payton, Jason Kidd, Ray Allen, Steve Smith, Tim Duncan, Tim Hardaway, Vin Baker, Vince Carter, and Shareef Abdur-Rahim.

Although the team won the gold medal, the victory was by no means easy. In fact, Team USA advanced to the gold-medal round in Sydney only after eking out a two-point win over Lithuania. In the championship game, the Americans defeated France by just 10 points.

In the two previous Olympics at which NBA stars had participated—the 1992 Summer Games in Barcelona, Spain, and the 1996 Summer Games in Atlanta—the American team had dominated. The 2000 results confirmed that the rest of the world was catching up to the United States in basketball.

Vince Carter (left) and Kevin Garnett show off their gold medals at the 2000 Summer Olympics in Sydney, Australia.

CROSS-CURRENTS

Helping the Victims of Hurricane Katrina

On August 29, 2005, Hurricane Katrina made landfall in the Gulf Coast of the United States. The massive storm devastated the region, including much of the popular historic city of New Orleans. Tens of thousands were forced from their homes.

Although many other celebrities contributed to the relief effort, Kevin Garnett's contribution was one of the most impressive. Through Oprah Winfrey's Angel Network foundation, Kevin donated $1.2 million to the rebuilding of homes for displaced victims.

Kevin even visited the victims and personally helped build several homes. "I heard Oprah's message about what people could do individually to help those affected by Hurricane Katrina," Kevin said, "and it made me think about what I could do. I'm glad to be partnering with an organization that is dedicated to making a difference, and through this project we are directly helping people who need it the most."

The NBA recognized Kevin's efforts to help the victims of Hurricane Katrina by giving him the 2006 J. Walter Kennedy Citizenship Award. That is the league's highest honor for service to the community.

NBA stars Cuttino Mobley (left) and Kevin Garnett hand out shoes to victims of Hurricane Katrina, September 2005.

CROSS-CURRENTS

Shaq and Kobe: Teammates and Rivals

The Los Angeles Lakers dominated the NBA in the first years of the 21st century, winning championships in 2000, 2001, and 2002. The team was loaded with talent, but two superstars stood out: Shaquille O'Neal and Kobe Bryant.

Standing 7'1" tall and weighing 325 pounds or more, O'Neal was considered the dominant center of his era. In each of the Lakers' championship seasons, O'Neal averaged more than 27 points and 10 rebounds per game. O'Neal was the Lakers' team captain and acknowledged leader on the floor.

However, the leadership role was one that Lakers guard Kobe Bryant thought he should play. Younger and flashier than Shaq, Kobe was capable of taking over games with his explosive offensive skills.

Despite the three championships they won together, Shaq and Kobe never got along. They often ridiculed each other in the media. Kobe once said Shaq was "fat and out of shape." He also said the big man displayed "childlike selfishness and jealousy." Shaq countered that Kobe was "a joke" and "a clown." In the summer of 2004, the bitter relationship came to an end when the Lakers traded Shaq to the Miami Heat.

Los Angeles Lakers teammates Shaquille O'Neal (left) and Kobe Bryant are all smiles during a 2000 game, but off the court the two carried on a long-running feud.

CROSS-CURRENTS

City of Champions

Boston, the largest city in Massachusetts, has four major professional sports teams: the Bruins in hockey, the Celtics in basketball, the Red Sox in baseball, and the New England Patriots in football. Before 2001, the city suffered a 15-year championship drought. But after the Patriots won Super Bowl XXVI on February 3, 2002, Boston's long-suffering sports fans had a whole lot to cheer about. Led by star quarterback Tom Brady, the Patriots won two more Super Bowls in the next three years.

In 2004, the Boston Red Sox finally broke a fabled championship drought that extended 86 long years. In 1918, Boston won its fifth World Series. But after the following season, the club sold the contract of a fine young pitcher who also showed a gift for hitting: Babe Ruth. This, superstitious Red Sox fans came to believe, led to "the Curse of the Bambino"; while Ruth's new team, the New York Yankees, went on to become baseball's most successful franchise, the Red Sox spent decade after decade in a futile quest to win another title. But after the 2004 Red Sox team ended the curse with a World Series win, Boston fans didn't have to wait long for another championship. The Red Sox won another World Series in 2007.

A year later, it was the Celtics' turn to bring another pro sports title to Boston. It was the sixth championship in nine years for the city.

Kevin Garnett fires up fans who turned out for the Boston Celtics 2008 victory parade.

Chronology

1976: Kevin Maurice Garnett is born on May 19 in Greenville, South Carolina.

1994: Named South Carolina's "Mr. Basketball." The family moves to Chicago.

1995: Kevin is named "Mr. Basketball" for Illinois. Selected fifth in the NBA draft by the Minnesota Timberwolves.

1997: Becomes the highest-paid athlete in American history when he signs a $126 million contract.

1998: Voted a starter on the NBA All-Star Team.

2000: Kevin's close friend Malik Sealy dies in a car accident in May. Kevin plays on the U.S. men's basketball team that wins the gold medal at the Olympics in Sydney, Australia.

2003: Kevin signs a $100 million extension to his contract.

2004: Kevin is named the NBA's Most Valuable Player. His Timberwolves team reaches the Western Conference Finals. He marries girlfriend Brandi Padilla.

2005: Donates $1.2 million to Hurricane Katrina relief efforts.

2007: Traded to the Boston Celtics.

2008: Wins Defensive Player of the Year honors. The Celtics capture the NBA championship.

Accomplishments/Awards

All-Rookie Second Team (1996)

NBA All-Star (1997, 1998, 2000, 2001, 2002, 2003, 2004, 2005, 2006, 2007, 2008)

All-NBA Third Team (1999, 2007)

All-NBA First Team (2000, 2003, 2004, 2008)

All-NBA Second Team (2001, 2002, 2005)

All-Star Game MVP (2003)

NBA MVP (2004)

Defensive Player of the Year (2008)

KEVIN GARNETT CAREER SEASON AVERAGES

Year	Team	G	GS	MPG	FG%	3P%	FT%	OFF	DEF	RPG	APG	SPG	BPG	TO	PF	PPG
95-96	MIN	80	43	28.7	0.491	0.286	0.705	2.2	4.1	6.3	1.8	1.1	1.6	1.38	2.4	10.4
96-97	MIN	77	77	38.9	0.499	0.286	0.754	2.5	5.6	8	3.1	1.4	2.1	2.27	2.6	17
97-98	MIN	82	82	39.3	0.491	0.188	0.738	2.7	6.9	9.6	4.2	1.7	1.8	2.34	2.7	18.5
98-99	MIN	47	47	37.9	0.46	0.286	0.704	3.5	6.9	10.4	4.3	1.7	1.8	2.87	3.2	20.8
99-00	MIN	81	81	40	0.497	0.37	0.765	2.8	9	11.8	5	1.5	1.6	3.31	2.5	22.9
00-01	MIN	81	81	39.5	0.477	0.288	0.764	2.7	8.7	11.4	5	1.4	1.8	2.84	2.5	22
01-02	MIN	81	81	39.2	0.47	0.319	0.801	3	9.1	12.1	5.2	1.2	1.6	2.83	2.3	21.2
02-03	MIN	82	82	40.5	0.502	0.282	0.751	3	10.5	13.4	6	1.4	1.6	2.79	2.4	23
03-04	MIN	82	82	39.4	0.499	0.256	0.791	3	10.9	13.9	5	1.5	2.2	2.59	2.5	24.2
04-05	MIN	82	82	38.1	0.502	0.24	0.811	3	10.5	13.5	5.7	1.5	1.4	2.71	2.5	22.2
05-06	MIN	76	76	38.9	0.526	0.267	0.81	2.8	9.9	12.7	4.1	1.4	1.4	2.37	2.7	21.8
06-07	MIN	76	76	39.4	0.476	0.214	0.835	2.4	10.4	12.8	4.1	1.2	1.7	2.7	2.4	22.4
07-08	BOS	71	71	32.8	0.539	0	0.801	1.9	7.3	9.2	3.4	1.4	1.2	1.94	2.3	18.8
CAREER	--	998	961	37.9	0.494	0.284	0.781	2.7	8.5	11.2	4.4	1.4	1.6	2.53	2.5	20.4
ALL-STAR	--	10	8	24.2	0.496	0	0.857	2.2	5.1	7.3	3.3	1.6	0.9	1.5	1	13.8

Further Reading

Finkel, Jon. *Greatest Stars of the NBA Volume 4: Kevin Garnett.* Los Angeles: TokyoPop, 2005.

Keith, Ted. *Kevin Garnett.* Mankato, MN: Child's World, 2007.

Stewart, Mark. *Kevin Garnett: Shake Up the Game.* Minneapolis, MN: Millbrook Press, 2002.

Internet Resources

http://www.boston.com

This Web site, run by the *Boston Globe*, provides up-to-the-minute information about Kevin Garnett and the Boston Celtics.

http://www.kevingarnett.com

Kevin Garnett's official Web site provides an in-depth look at the athlete's life.

http://www.sportsillustrated.com

Sports Illustrated magazine's Web site contains years of stories about Kevin Garnett's life and career.

Publisher's Note: The Web sites listed on this page were active at the time of publication. The publisher is not responsible for Web sites that have changed their address or discontinued operation since the date of publication. The publisher reviews and updates the Web sites each time the book is reprinted.

Glossary

consecutive—following one another in order without interruption.

draft—the method by which young players are selected to play in a professional sports league such as the NBA.

franchise—an organization that owns a team.

free agent—a player who is not currently under contract to play for a team, and who may therefore negotiate with any team he chooses.

lockout—a refusal by business owners to permit their employees to work, as a means of pressuring the employees to agree to certain terms (such as wages).

rookie—a player in his first year.

scout—in basketball, a person employed by a team to find talented high school, college, and other players who might be drafted by the team.

unanimous—in complete agreement.

veteran—a player who has played for many years.

Chapter Notes

p. 8: "I got my own . . ." Associated Press, "Celtics Smash Lakers, Bring Home 17th NBA Championship," ESPN.com. http://scores.espn.go.com/nba/recap?gameId=280617002

p. 8: "You sure did." Ibid.

p. 8: "Put simply, Garnett shrinks . . ." Bill Simmons, "Let's Play Word Association: KG. Warrior? Sure. 2008 MVP? Maybe. Clutch? Eh.," ESPN The Magazine, 2008. http://sports.espn.go.com/espnmag/story?id=3403820

p. 8: "Other than my kid . . ." Quoted in Scoop Jackson, "The Game of His Life," ESPN.com, June 18, 2008. http://sports.espn.go.com/espn/print?id=3450696&type=story

p. 9: "There is this amazing . . ." Mike Kahn, "Lakers-Celtics Finals Will Come down to Kobe," Fox Sports on MSN, June 5, 2008. http://msn.foxsports.com/nba/story/8207852/Lakers-Celtics-finals-will-come-down-to-Kobe

p. 10: "The defense is our backbone . . ." Quoted in John Schuhmann, "Boston Celtics—2008 NBA Finals Champs," TV20DETROIT.com, June 18, 2008. http://www.tv20detroit.com/sports/20428964.html

p. 12: "I've always had a job . . ." Scoop Jackson, "*Hoop* Magazine: The Man," NBA.com, May 16, 2006. http://www.nba.com/features/hoop_kg_040219.html

Chapter Notes

p. 13: "All he did . . ." Ellen Tomson, "Kevin Garnett: Passion Play," *St. Paul Pioneer Press*, November 30, 1997. http://www.cyberhood.info/et/garnett.html

p. 13: "I'm an advocate . . ." J. Chris Roselius, *Kevin Garnett: All-Star On and Off the Court* (Berkeley Heights, N.J.: Enslow Publishers, 2008), 19.

p. 13: "When I didn't . . ." Bob Carter, "'Da Kid' Progressed Quickly," ESPN.com, May 10, 2006. http://espn.go.com/classic/biography/s/Garnett_Kevin.html

p. 14: "I knew he was gifted . . ." Joe Gioia, "The $126 Million Man," Salon.com, February 12, 2000. http://archive.salon.com/people/feature/2000/02/12/garnett/index.html

p. 14: "I don't think . . ." Carter, "'Da Kid.'"

p. 15: "Kevin could have . . ." Roselius, *Kevin Garnett*, 26.

p. 16: "At the time . . ." Frank Clancy, "The Kid's All Right," *Sporting News*, March 4, 1996. http://findarticles.com/p/articles/mi_m1208/is_n10_v220/ai_18064184/pg_3

p. 19: "First of all . . ." Michael Wilbon, "For Prep Star Garnett, NBA Is Fool's Gold," *Washington Post*, May 28, 1995.

p. 19: "Is Kevin Garnett ready . . ." Jay Mariotti, "Does Garnett Have Any Idea of What He Is Getting Into?", *Chicago Sun-Times*, June 20, 1995.

p. 24: "Who would have ever . . ." Carter, "'Da Kid' Progressed."

p. 26: "I know [Malik's] gone . . ." Roselius, *Kevin Garnett*, 78.

p. 28: "So many young . . ." "Kevin Garnett Launches 4XL," February 18, 2002. http://www.kevingarnett.com/4xl_archive.aspx

p. 29: "man who had multimillions . . ." Jackson, "The Man."

Chapter Notes

p. 31: "Anybody mess this up . . ." Jeff Lenchiner, "Kevin Garnett Interview," InsideHoops.com, October 15, 2003. http://www.insidehoops.com/garnett-interview-101503.shtml

p. 31: "Kevin McHale and myself . . ." "Flip Saunders Interview," InsideHoops.com, October 27, 2004. http://www.insidehoops.com/saunders-interview-102704.shtml

p. 31: "I've never met . . ." Jackson, "The Man."

p. 32: "My goals are a lot . . ." Brandt Williams, "Garnett Named MVP of NBA," Minnesota Public Radio, May 3, 2004. http://news.minnesota.publicradio.org/features/2004/05/03_williamsb_kgmvp/

p. 32: "I am very excited . . ." Roselius, Kevin Garnett, 101.

p. 34: "I got a taste . . ." Greg Beacham, "Lakers Fab Four Advance to NBA Finals," *Oakland Tribune*, June 1, 2004. http://findarticles.com/p/articles/mi_qn4176/is_20040601/ai_n14575431

p. 36: "This is a tremendous . . ." Marc Stein, "Five Players, Two Picks Sent to Wolves for Garnett," ESPN.com, August 1, 2007. http://sports.espn.go.com/nba/news/story?id=2956103

p. 36: "This is probably . . ." Ibid.

p. 36: "These guys will . . ." Ibid.

p. 38: "was so hyped . . ." Bob Ryan, "Big Night No Big Deal for Garnett," Boston.com, November 3, 2007. http://www.boston.com/sports/basketball/celtics/articles/2007/11/03/big_night_no_big_deal_for_garnett/

p. 39: "We didn't execute . . ." Ibid.

Chapter Notes

p. 39: "It's about what you're able . . ." "Kevin Garnett: The Complete Package," *Boston Herald*, June 20, 2008. http://www.bostonherald.com/sports/basketball/celtics/a_banner_year/view.bg?articleid=1101710

p. 40: "Garnett completely altered . . ." Ibid.

p. 41: "Any award you're able . . ." "Garnett Named Defensive Player of the Year," TSN, April 22, 2008. http://www.tsn.ca/nba/story/?id=235474

p. 41: "He's changed our culture . . ." Ibid.

p. 44: "Garnett finished with . . ." Bill Simmons, "Notes from a Good Ol' Fashion Garden Party," ESPN.com, June 18, 2008. http://sports.espn.go.com/espn/page2/story?page=simmons/080618

p. 47: "This is unreal just . . ." "NBA Finals: Lakers v Celtics," ASAP Sports, June 17, 2008. http://www.asapsports.com/show_interview.php?id=50260

p. 47: "It was a shock . . ." David Aldridge, "Pierce, Walker Can't Forget the Violence," ESPN.com, January 4, 2001. http://espn.go.com/nba/columns/aldridge/993704.html

p. 51: "I heard Oprah's . . ." "Kevin Garnett Announces Hurricane Katrina Assistance," November 10, 2005. http://www.nba.com/timberwolves/community/garnett_oprah_051110.html

Index

Abdul-Jabbar, Kareem, 46
Abdur-Rahim, Shareef, 50
Ainge, Danny, 9, 36
Allen, Ray, 8, 9, *34*, 35, 36–37, *43*, 50
Amateur Athletic Union (AAU), 14, 15

Baker, Vin, 50
Baylor, Elgin, 46
"Big Ticket" (nickname), 31
   See also Garnett, Kevin
Bird, Larry, 8, 36–37, 46
Blair, Bill, 20–21
Boston Celtics, 37–44
   championship wins of, 6–11, 42–44, 46–47, 53
   and the playoffs, 41–42
   trade for Garnett, *34*, 35–36
   See also Garnett, Kevin
Brandon, Terrell, 24
Bryant, Kobe, 9, 33, 42, 48, 52

Carter, Vince, 50
Cassell, Sam, 31–32
Chamberlain, Wilt, 46
charity work, 27–29, 45, 51
Clancy, Frank, 16
Cousy, Bob, 8, 46

"Da Kid" (nickname), 20
   See also Garnett, Kevin
Dawkins, Darryl, 48
Defensive Player of the Year award, 10, 41
draft, NBA, 17–20, 45, 48
Duncan, Tim, 29, 50

Farragut Academy, 16–17

Fisher, James, 14
Fleisher, Eric, 21
4XL, 28–29
Franks, Baron, 13

Garnett, Kevin
   awards and honors won by, 10, 15, 17, 21, 27, 29, 32, 41, 51
   birth and childhood, 12–13
   with the Boston Celtics, 6–11, *34*, 35–44
   and charity work, 27–29, 45, 51
   as Defensive Player of the Year, 10, 41
   at Farragut Academy, 16–17
   and injuries, 40
   and legal troubles, 15–16
   at Mauldin High School, 14–15
   with the Minnesota Timberwolves, 8, 20–27, 29–34
   as "Mr. Basketball," 15, 17
   and the NBA draft, 17–20, 45, 48
   as NBA MVP, 32
   nicknames, 20, 31
   and the Olympics, 26, 50
   salary, 21–22, 31
   statistics, 20, 21, 22, 24, 27, 29, 32, 33, 34, 38, 39, 42, 43
Garnett, Shirley (mother), 12, 13, 16, *17*, 19
Gazaway, Darren ("Bull"), 15
Gugliotta, Tom, 20, 21

Hardaway, Tim, 50
Havlicek, John, 8, 46
Hopkins, Stan, 14
Houston, Allan, 50

Irby, Ernest (stepfather), 12

Numbers in **bold italics** refer to captions.

Index

J. Walter Kennedy Citizenship Award, 51
Jackson, Scoop, 29
James, LeBron, 42, 48
Jefferson, Al, 35
Johnson, Magic, 21, 46

Kahn, Mike, 9
Kidd, Jason, 50

Laettner, Christian, 20
Lewis, Reggie, 49
Los Angeles Lakers, 6, 8–10, 29–30, 33–34, 39, 42–43, 46, 52

Malone, Moses, 48
Marbury, Stephon, 21, 24
Mariotti, Jay, 19
Mauldin High School, 14–15
McCullough, O'Lewis (father), 12
McDyess, Antonio, 50
McGrady, Tracy, 48
McHale, Kevin, 8, 18, 20–21, 31, 36–37, 46
Minnesota Timberwolves, 8, 20–27, 29–34, 40
  draft Garnett, 18
  and the playoffs, 21, 22, 24–25, 27, 29–30, 32–34
  See also Garnett, Kevin
Most Valuable Player (MVP) award, 32
Mourning, Alonzo, 50
"Mr. Basketball" awards, 15, 17

National Basketball Association (NBA)
  draft, 17–20, 45, 48
  lockout (1998), 23
Nelson, William (Wolf), 16–17

Olympics, 26, 50
O'Neal, Jermaine, 48
O'Neal, Shaquille, 33, 52

Parish, Robert, 36–37, 46
Payton, Gary, 50
Peters, Jamie ("Bug"), 13
Petrovic, Drazen, 49
Pierce, Paul, 8, 9, 10–11, **34**, 35, 36–37, **43**, 47

Rivers, Doc, 38, 41
Russell, Bill, 8, 46

Saunders, Phil "Flip," 21, 31
Sealy, Malik, 25–26, 49
Simmons, Bill, 8, 43–44
Smith, Steve, 50
Sprewell, Latrell, 31, 34
Stoudemire, Amare, 48
Szczerbiak, Wally, 24

Tafoya, Michele, 6
Taylor, Glen, 21, 35
Tomson, Ellen, 13

Walton, Bill, 24
Webber, Chris, **23**, 32
West, Jerry, 46
Wilbon, Michael, 19
Willoughby, Bill, 48
Worthy, James, 46

Photo Credits

- 7: Elsa/Getty Images
- 10: Brian Babineau/NBAE via Getty Images
- 13: © 2008 Jupiterimages Corporation
- 14: Carl Sissac/Time Life Pictures/Getty Images
- 16: Carl Sissac/Time Life Pictures/Getty Images
- 17: Tim Chevrier/NBAE via Getty Images
- 20: Dale Dait/NBAE via Getty Images
- 23: Andrew D. Bernstein/NBAE/Getty Images
- 25: (left) Craig Lassig/AFP/Getty Images; (right) AP Photo/Mark Lennihan
- 28: David Sherman/NBAE via Getty Images
- 30: David Sherman/NBAE via Getty Images
- 31: David Sherman/NBAE via Getty Images
- 33: Noah Graham/NBAE via Getty Images
- 34: AP Photo/Steven Senne
- 37: Brian Babineau/NBAE via Getty Images
- 38: Brian Babineau/NBAE via Getty Images
- 40: Brian Babineau/NBAE via Getty Images
- 43: Brian Babineau/NBAE via Getty Images
- 44: Gabriel Bouys/AFP/Getty Images
- 46: Andrew D. Bernstein/NBAE/Getty Images
- 47: Gabriel Bouys/AFP/Getty Images
- 48: AP Photo/Robert Houston
- 49: Jon SooHoo/NBAE via Getty Images
- 50: Jamie Squire/Allsport/Getty Images
- 51: Garrett Ellwood/NBAE via Getty Images
- 52: Andrew D. Bernstein/NBAE via Getty Images
- 53: Brian Babineau/NBAE via Getty Images

Cover Images:
Main Image: POOL/AFP/Getty Images
Top Inset: Noah Graham/NBAE/Getty Images
Bottom Inset: Joe Murphy/NBAE/Getty Images

About the Author

JAMIE FEDORKO is the award-winning author of *The Intern Files: How to Get, Keep and Make the Most of Your Internship*. Born and raised in New York and an avid sports fan, Fedorko has worked with such publications as *GQ, Vibe, Paper,* and *Laptop* magazines as well as with CNBC Networks. This is his third book.

FEB 17 2010
22⁹⁵

DISCARD